MARC BROWN

Sir Arthur to the Rescue

"ACTORS NEEDED FOR ELWOOD CITY CHILDREN'S THEATER," the sign read in big letters.

"I want to be Queen Guinevere," said Muffy.

"A palace guard sounds good to me," said Buster. "Who do you want to try for, Arthur?"

"Who else?" he said. "King Arthur!"

At the auditions, Arthur met the director, the legendary soap opera actress Ivanna Starr.

"You with the glasses," said Miss Starr. "I will hear you read now."

Arthur took a deep breath and sat down on the throne. "I am the mighty Arthur, ruler of Cantaloupe...er, I mean, Camelot," he said.

"That will be all," said Miss Starr.

The following day, Miss Starr posted the cast list.

"I'm the queen!" squealed Muffy.

"Cool!" said Binky. "I'm a knight!"

"I'm a lady-in-waiting," said Prunella.

CAST LIST

KING ARTHUR – BUSTER BAXTER

GUINEVERE – MUFFY CROSSWIRE

KNIGHT – BINKY BARNES

LADY-IN-WAITING – PRUNELLA

STABLE BOY – ARTHUR

Arthur spotted the role of King Arthur. It read "Buster Baxter."

"Attention, cast!" Miss Starr interrupted. "Here are your scripts."

"Arthur, you'll be playing the stable boy," said Miss Starr. "And remember...there are no small parts, only small actors!"

The first week of rehearsals was rough. Binky couldn't walk in his armor and Muffy hated her gown.

"Why can't it be pink?" she said.

"This king stuff is great!" said Buster. He loved pulling the sword out of a large fake stone.

"What's wrong with you, Buster?" asked Binky.

"What do you mean?" said Buster. "I'm the big star!"

"No way!" insisted Binky. "I'm bigger than you!"

"You tell him, Binky," said Arthur.

"You're just jealous," Buster said. "Because I'm playing King Arthur and you're not."

"I liked you better as Buster," Arthur said softly.

Soon Buster started to believe he really was royalty.

"Make way," he said. "The king is coming through."

"Oh, brother," Prunella said.

The next week was worse. Buster insisted on a chair that had his name on it. He even handed out autographs.

"Just think," said Buster. "You knew me before I was famous!"

Later that day, Buster had a rough time.

"You must surrender to the great King Buster...er, Arthur," said Buster.

"You need to learn your lines," said Miss Starr.

"No problem," said Buster. "Just wait till we open!"

The big night finally arrived. The theater was packed.

Buster peeked out from behind the curtain and gulped.

"That's a lot of people," he said nervously.

"Yes, and they're all waiting to see you," said Miss Starr.

When the curtain rose, Buster just stood and stared at the audience.

"He has stage fright!" cried Miss Starr. "He's ruining my production! Someone do something!"

Arthur had an idea.

"O mighty King," he called.
"You must pull the sword
from the stone."

But Buster didn't budge.
Neither did the sword.

So Arthur picked up a tree
and sneaked across the stage.

"Pssst, Buster," he whispered.
"Calm down. You can do it."

Soon Buster began to relax a little and the
words came to him.

"Um...I claim the sword Excalibur!" he shouted,
pulling the sword from the stone.

When the show ended, the audience thundered with applause and cheers.

At the curtain call, Miss Starr blew kisses to the audience.

Buster got a standing ovation.

Suddenly Buster pulled Arthur onstage.

The audience cheered. Arthur felt really proud.

"Take a bow," said Buster. "You deserve it."

"Thanks," whispered Buster. "You really saved me."

"That's what best friends are for," whispered Arthur.